Dear Reader,

"This book will enchant and uplift children
of the heart no matter their age!

How wonderful to find a children's book that brings
Winter Solstice more fully into one's purview! This holiday story
introduces whimsical characters that capture the most endearing
of human qualities with heartwarming stories of bravery, kindness,
acceptance and love. I was enchanted by the luscious wool
illustrations that bring this book to life, and the poetic language
that moves the story along."

~ Robin White Turtle Lysne, Ph.D. Blue Bone Books, Santa Cruz, CA Author of
Dancing Up the Moon, Sacred Living and Heart Path, Heart Path Handbook.

A Winter Solstice TALE

Would You Unquestionably Rather Be Yourself?

Amma Sharon

'Twas a chilly Winter Solstice Eve

in the enchanted, woodland dell of Happy Hollow.

Snappy, the curious woodland Gnome,

Furry Mouse, Miss Bunny, and Bear busily prepared

for their traditional celebration to follow.

Buzzing with mid-winter magic and good cheer,

the merry band of woodland friends

make ready for the longest night of the year.

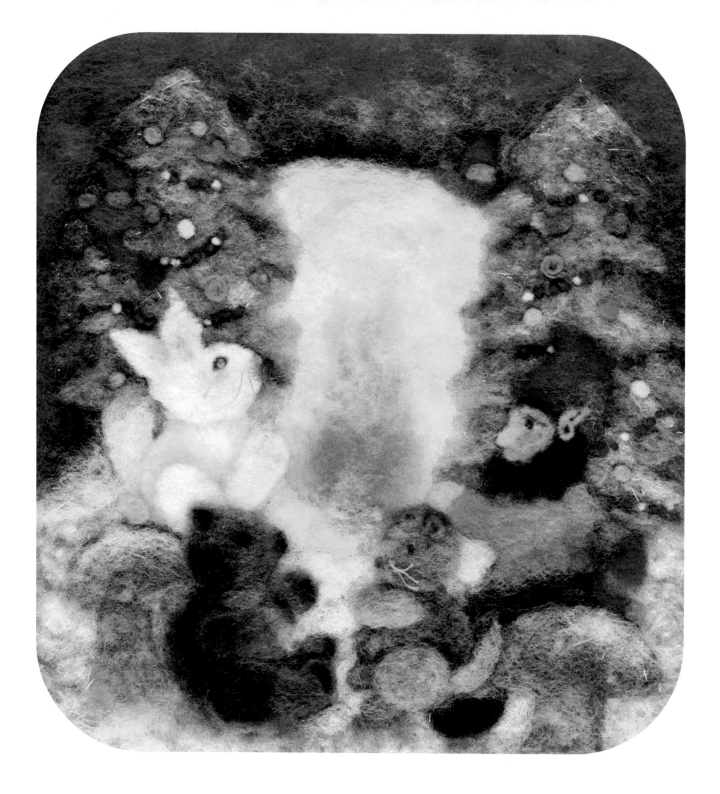

Around the crackling Yule fire

with mulled cider and Solstice fare,

the merry friends celebrate midwinter

with heartwarming stories to share.

Sprightly adventures

told in sweet sounding rhyme

about their year that had passed

through the hands of time.

Evergreen trees shimmered

like tinsel, layered in snowy white.

Billowy snow clouds played tag with Solstice Moon,

drenching Night Sky with peekaboo light.

Solstice Moon, so enchanting and so wonderfully round,

watched as the eager friends settled

on the snow painted ground.

At the edge of the glade,

just out of sight,

Christmas Elves in red velvet

danced ever so light, as Elves do

when they listen

to stories in the night!

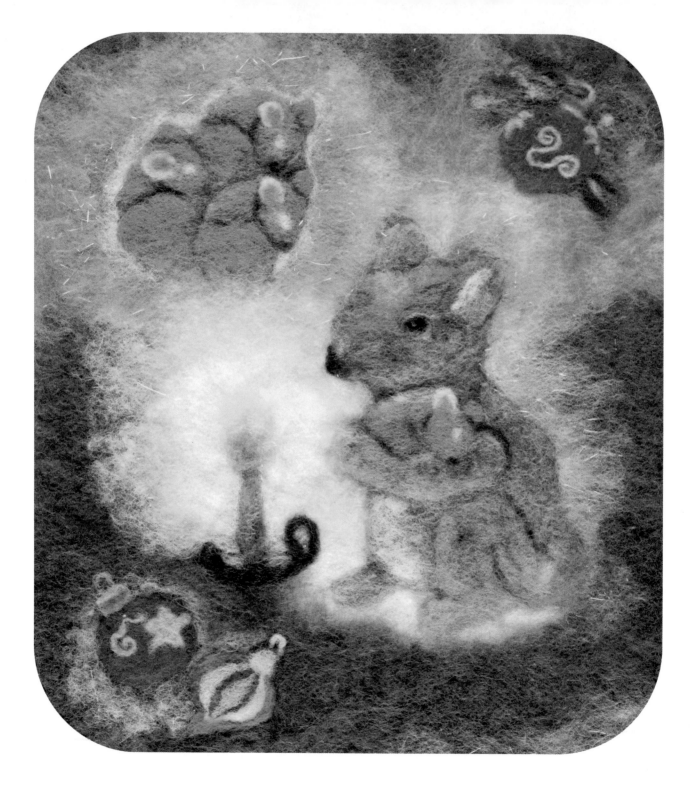

With whimsical charm Furry Mouse

squeaked a dear tale,

about her mouskin adventure

fetching sweetgrass,

with her strong mousy tail.

Her mouse pups soon nestled in freshly made beds,

the aroma of sweetgrass swirling 'round in their heads.

Furry lulled them with mid-winter magic that night,

by the flickering, woodsy scent of pale candlelight.

Drifting snugly into slumber her mousy pups fell.

Furry glowed as she watched them

and her mother's heart swelled!

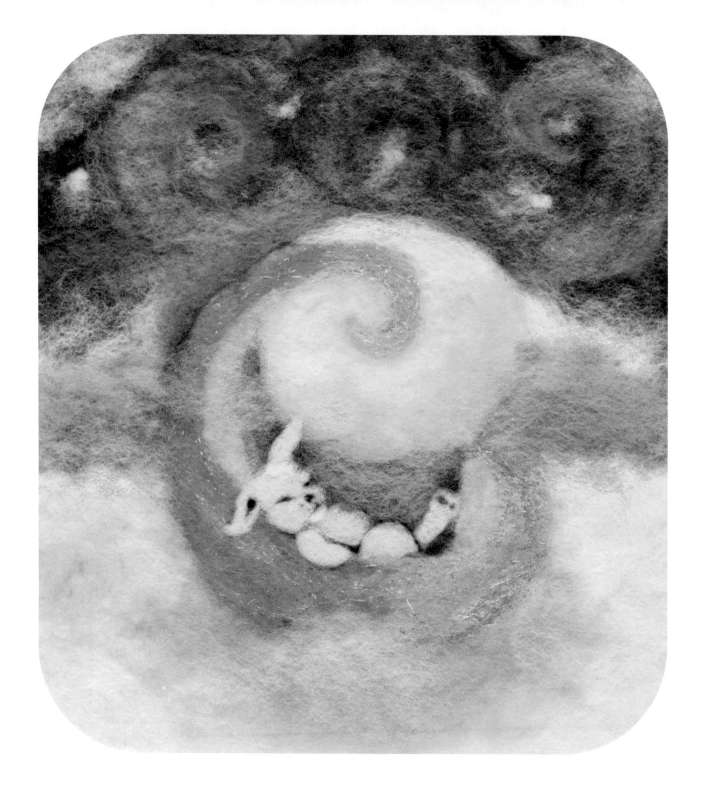

Miss Bunny chirruped her story

about wishing on a falling star,

to sail beside the Milky Way

over lands near and far.

As if by magic, a glittering moonbeam appeared

to sail Miss Bunny away.

Oh! the grand story she wove by the crackling Yule fire

of her wonderous adventure in a moonbeam sleigh.

Bear's story caused the others to whistle!

Bravely, Bear carried a hoglet

across a river of ice crystals.

On the far riverbank

a worried hedgehog family stood by,

cheering Bear onward to reach the other side.

All were grateful, thankful, and happy

for Bear's courage in the dark.

Mother Hedgehog scooped up her wet hoglet,

snuggling it close to her heart.

Snappy's story came last, but not least

as they say! A happenstance meeting

one sun-drenched winter's day.

Snappy was drawn toward Rock Elf,

on a trek from up North. He lay sprawled

on a river rock, seeking sun warmth.

Snappy asked Rock Elf, *"If you could be anyone,*

who would you rather be?"

"If I could be anyone," replied the wise, timeworn Elf,

"I would unquestionably rather be myself!"

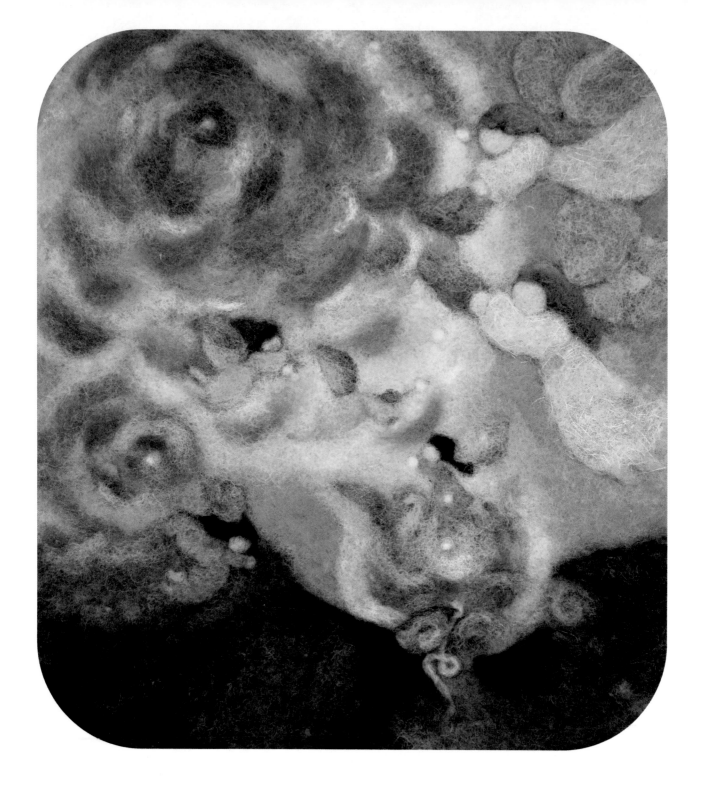

Rock Elf smartly went on to explain,

"When a rose seed is planted

that little seed knows, to become a rosebush,

only its rosy self can grow.

Buried in the earth until rain, sun, and starry night,

wake the sleeping seed with conditions just right!"

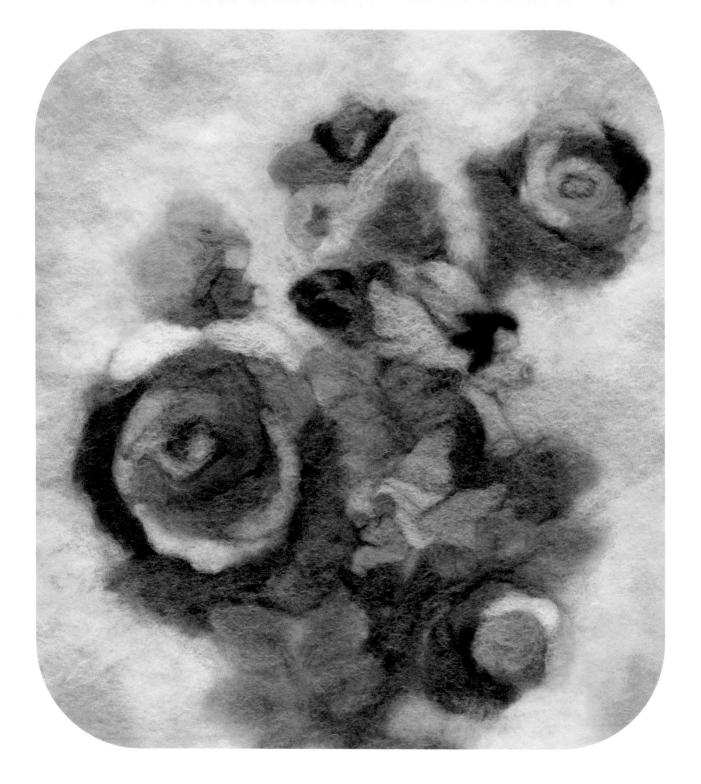

As if by magic, a Solstice Rose appeared,

with rainbow petals, one of a kind, it was clear.

While sun-soaked Rock Elf and Snappy breathed

the rosy sweetness filling the air,

Rock Elf continued with more insights to share,

"Inside you lives a 'knowing',

— unlike any other —

ready to unfold with so much to discover!"

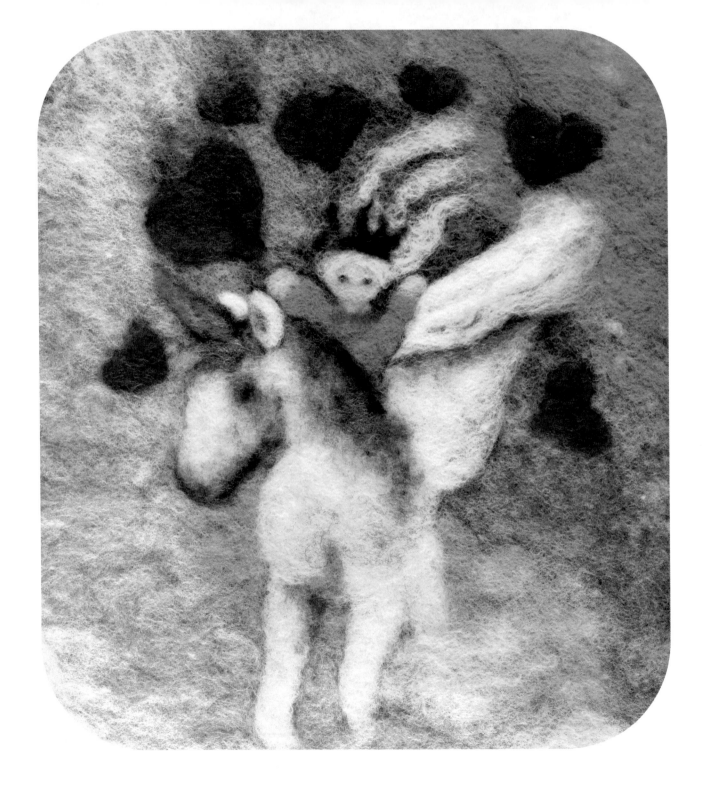

There is only one of you, unique in every way!

So, if someone ever asks you

on a sun-drenched winter's day,

— or any other —

"Who would you rather be?"

I trust you will say, like wise Rock Elf,

"I would unquestionably rather be myself!"

Snappy treasured the rich lesson,

it lived within him all his days!

He gratefully hugged Rock Elf before warmly parting ways.

Rock Elf hugged the rock's sun-soaked, granite dome

that had warmed his outstretched,

sun-seeking, elven bones.

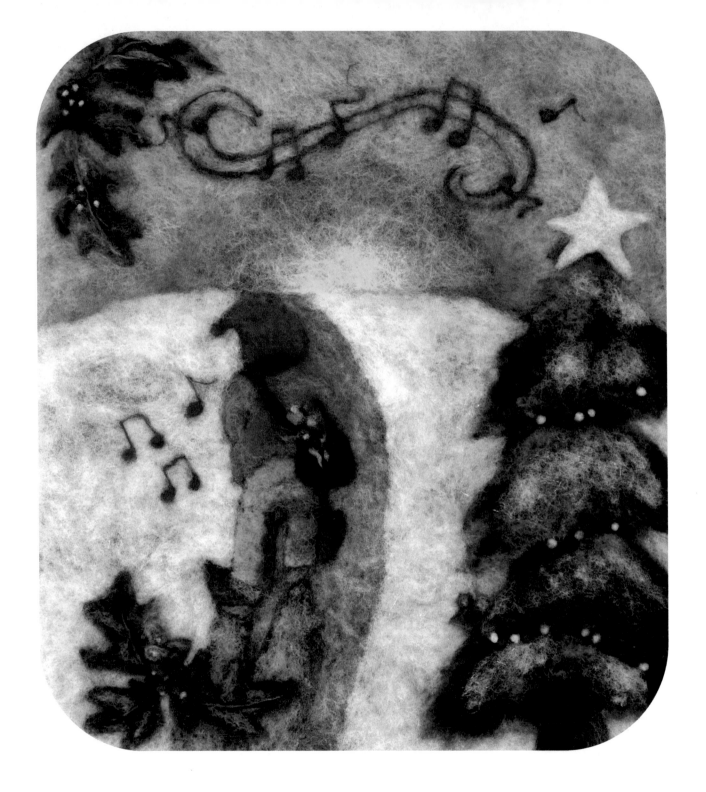

Happy Solstice and glad tidings

from Snappy, Furry Mouse, Miss Bunny, and Bear.

May the magic of mid-winter

warm your hearts throughout the new year!

As Snappy skipped homeward

he heard jingling bells fill the night.

A Ho! Ho! Ho! called from somewhere out of sight,

I celebrate the life that expresses itself through,
— Uniquely Amazing, Lovable YOU! —

Other books in the Happy Hollow Children's Series by Amma Sharon

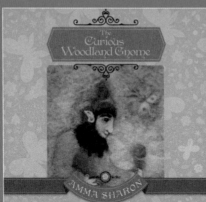

A Winter Solstice Tale
'Would You Unquestionably Rather be Yourself?'

Winter solstice is joyously celebrated in the magical woodland dell of Happy Hollow.
Uplifting stories of bravery, friendship, and love are shared around the crackling night fire.

Copyright © 2020 Amma Sharon Fletter- Sharon Fletter
Copyright © 2020 Felted Illustrations Amma Sharon Fletter- Sharon Fletter
ISBN: (hc) 978-1-7361222-0-4
ISBN: (paperback)

Cover Designs by Roseanna M. White. www.RoseannaWhiteDesigns.com

www.ammasharonstories.com

Made in the USA
Middletown, DE
24 November 2021

53365203R00018